The Best Gifts

The Best Gifts

Marsha Forchuk Skrypuch

ILLUSTRATED BY

Elly MacKay

Fitzhenry & Whiteside

Published in Canada by Fitzhenry & Whiteside, 195 Allstate Parkway, Markham, Ontario L3R 4T8
Published in the United States by Fitzhenry & Whiteside, 311 Washington Street, Brighton, Massachusetts 02135

www.fitzhenry.ca   godwit@fitzhenry.ca

10 9 8 7 6 5 4 3 2 1

Library and Archives Canada Cataloguing in Publication
Skrypuch, Marsha Forchuk, 1954-
The best gifts / Marsha Forchuk Skrypuch ; illustrated
by Elly MacKay.
ISBN 978-1-55455-283-2 (bound)
I. MacKay, Elly II. Title.
PS8587.K79B47 2013   jC813'.54   C2013-902038-1
Publisher Cataloging-in-Publication Data (U.S.)
Skrypuch, Marsha Forchuk.
The best gifts / Marsha Forchuk Skrypuch ; illustrated by Elly MacKay.
[32] p. : col. ill. ; cm.
Includes index.
Summary: The story of important moments in the life of a girl that starts with her birth and concludes when she
welcomes her own baby; showing that the most cherished gifts are the ones that cannot be purchased. The first
cherished gift the girl receives is her mother's milk, and the story comes full circle when she gives the same gift to
her own baby.
ISBN: 978-1-55455-283-2
1. Gifts – Juvenile fiction. 2. Mother and child – Juvenile fiction. I. MacKay, Elly. II. Title.
[E] dc23 PZ7.S579be 2013
Fitzhenry & Whiteside acknowledges with thanks the Canada Council for the Arts, and the Ontario Arts Council
for their support of our publishing program. We acknowledge the financial support of the Government of Canada
through the Canada Book Fund (CBF) for our publishing activities.

ONTARIO ARTS COUNCIL
CONSEIL DES ARTS DE L'ONTARIO
50 YEARS OF ONTARIO GOVERNMENT SUPPORT OF THE ARTS
50 ANS DE SOUTIEN DU GOUVERNEMENT DE L'ONTARIO AUX ARTS

Canada Council
for the Arts
Conseil des Arts
du Canada

Cover and interior design by Daniel Choi
Cover illustration by Elly MacKay

Printed in China by Sheck Wah Tong Printing Press Ltd.

To Mom
–Marsha Forchuk Skrypuch

To my beautiful children
–Elly McKay

With thanks to Mahtab Narsimhan and Sampa Bhadra

When Sara was born, friends and family welcomed her with joy and special gifts. Her parents opened the gifts and thanked everyone for their thoughtfulness.

When all the visitors had left, Sara's father put the gifts away. Then he sat on the bed as Sara's mother opened her nightgown and drew their daughter near. Sara was wrapped in love and a light scent of sandalwood as the warmth of her mother's milk swirled in her mouth and filled her tiny stomach. She fell into a happy sleep.

On Sara's fifth birthday, friends and family celebrated with joy and special gifts. Sara opened the gifts and thanked everyone for their thoughtfulness.

When all the visitors had left, Sara's parents helped her put the gifts away. Then Sara's father took out a love-worn story book that he had treasured since he was little. Sara's parents took turns reading it aloud to her.

Sara was wrapped in love and comfort as the words swirled around her mind. It didn't matter so much what the story was; it was who was doing the reading. Sara fell into a happy sleep.

When Sara finished school, friends and family gathered round with joy and special gifts. Sara opened the gifts and thanked everyone for their thoughtfulness.

When all the visitors had left, Sara and her parents packed the gifts into her suitcase. Sara knew that she was no longer a little girl, and that she was ready for her next adventure.

But she was already missing home.

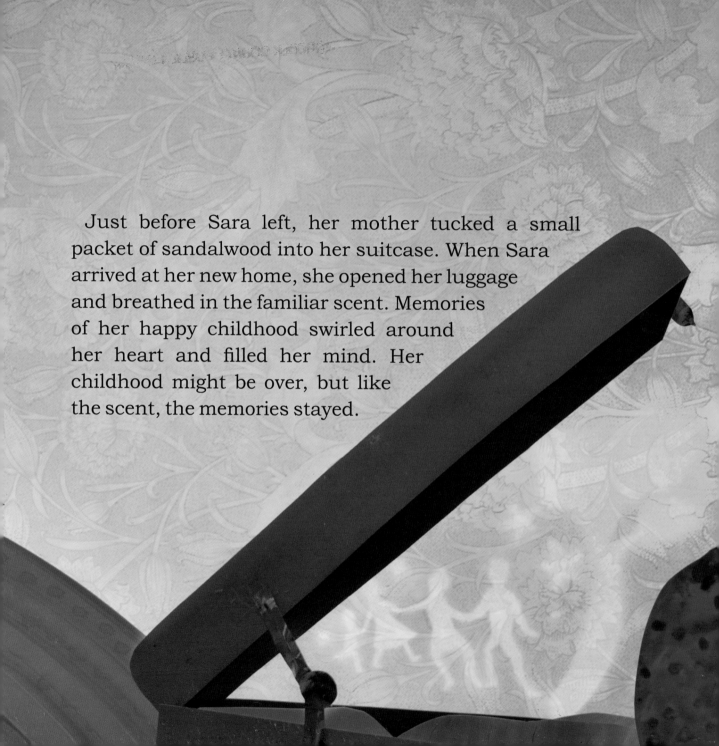

Just before Sara left, her mother tucked a small packet of sandalwood into her suitcase. When Sara arrived at her new home, she opened her luggage and breathed in the familiar scent. Memories of her happy childhood swirled around her heart and filled her mind. Her childhood might be over, but like the scent, the memories stayed.

After years on her own, Sara found
her one true love. On her wedding day,
friends and family gathered round with joy and
special gifts. Sara and her husband opened their gifts
and thanked everyone for their thoughtfulness.

When all the visitors had left, Sara's parents helped the newlyweds put the gifts away, and then they gave a gift of their own. It was a photo album covered with fabric from Sara's baby blanket.

Sara's parents had filled the album with photographs of Sara growing up. There were pictures of her new husband too, growing up with his parents. Sara's heart was filled with love and warmth. She kissed each parent on the cheek, then took her husband's hand, thankful for what she had.

Years later, Sara and her husband had a baby of their own. Friends and family gathered with joy and special gifts for baby Sam. Sara and her husband opened the gifts and thanked everyone for their thoughtfulness.

One by one, the visitors left. The last to leave were Sara's parents, who gave to her the love-worn story book. She knew how much they treasured it and they knew how much Sam would love it. Sara wrapped her arms around her parents' shoulders and kissed them each on the cheek. Then they left.

Sara's husband put the gifts away. Then he sat on the bed next to Sara as she opened her nightgown and drew their child near.

Sam was wrapped in love and a light scent of sandalwood as the warmth of his mother's milk swirled in his mouth and filled his tiny stomach. He fell into a happy sleep.

And Sara knew, as she always had…

…that the best gifts can never be bought.

The Best Gifts

Breastfeeding resources

"Breastfeeding is the normal way of providing young infants with the nutrients they need for healthy growth and development. Virtually all mothers can breastfeed, provided they have accurate information, and the support of their family, the health care system and society at large."
—World Health Organization.

To find a breastfeeding support group near you:

La Leche League International

"Our Mission is to help mothers worldwide to breastfeed through mother-to-mother support, encouragement, information, and education, and to promote a better understanding of breastfeeding as an important element in the healthy development of the baby and mother."
www.llli.org

To learn more about breastfeeding and health:

The International Baby Food Action Network
IBFAN: Defending Breastfeeding
A worldwide network that promotes breastfeeding for the optimal health of babies and young children.
www.ibfan.org

World Health Organization
http://www.who.int/topics/breastfeeding